Just Think!

by Bette Killion

pictures by

"Come quickly," says my mother
or some other hurry-up person.

Then I think of fast things—

hummingbird wings

lizards darting

racers starting

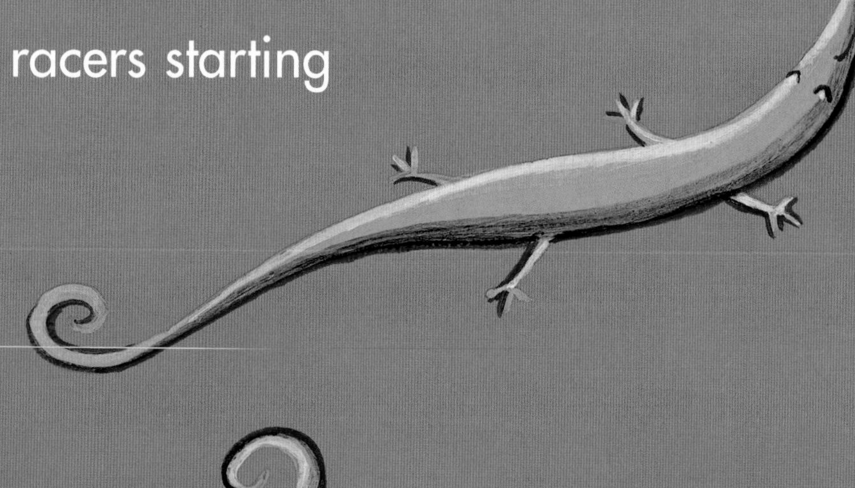

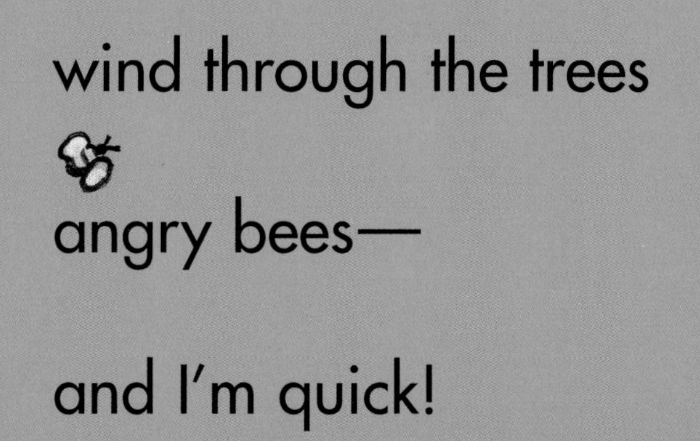

wind through the trees

angry bees—

and I'm quick!

"Slow down!"
says my mother
or some other
poke-along person.

Then I think of lazy things—

trailing strings

elephants strolling

a plump pig rolling

sipping lemonade

sitting in the shade—

and I'm slow.

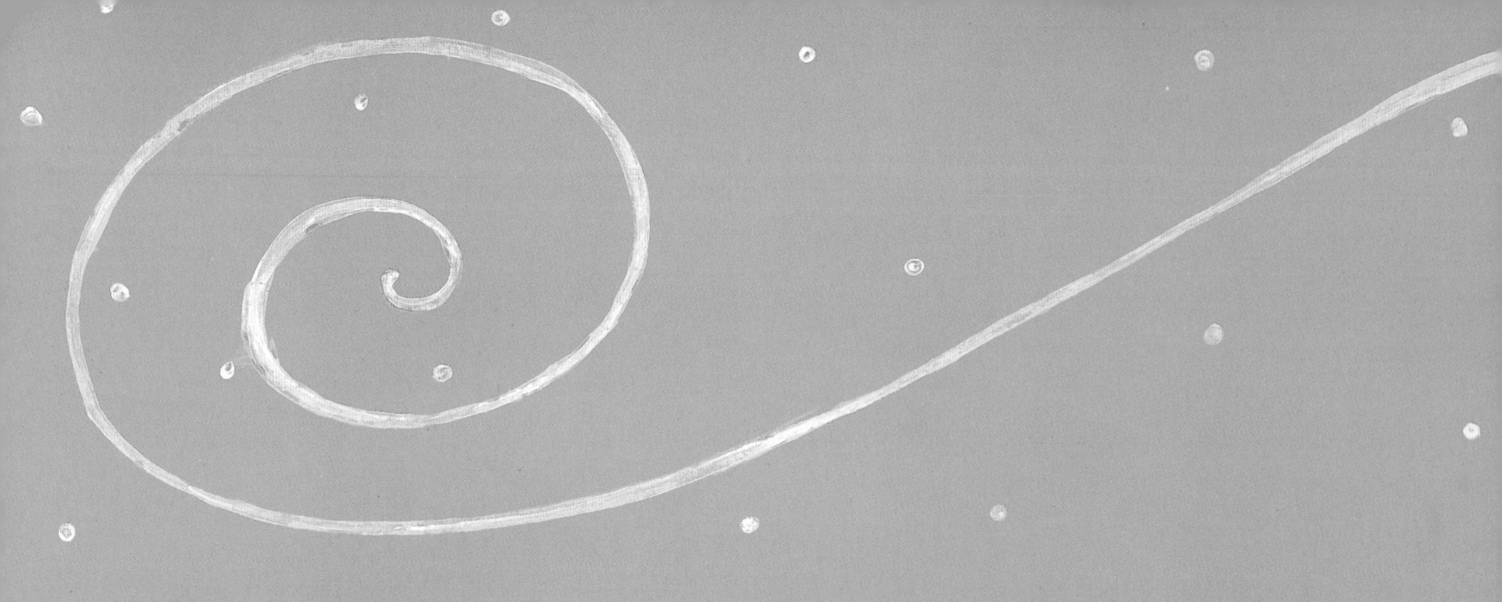

"Shh! Be quiet!" says my mother
or some other tiptoe person.

Then I think of still things—

empty swings

snow drifting high

first star in the sky

cuddly bears

whispered prayers—

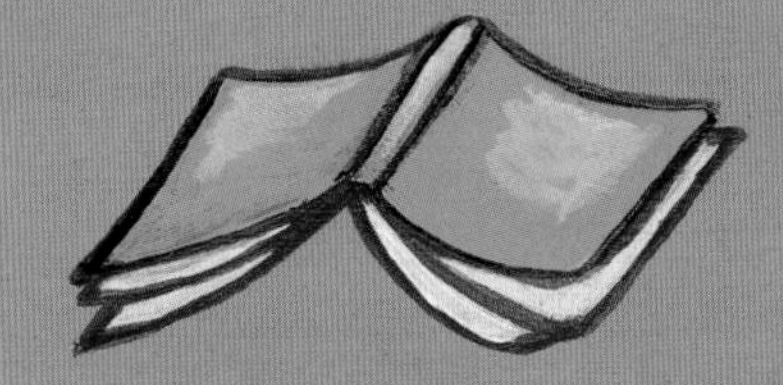